Addison and the Aliens

Sunny Cabana Publishing, L.L.C.

Broomfield, CO

www.sunnycabanapublishing.com

facebook.com/sunnycabanapublishing

Authored by Kathy Tennefoss

Illustrations by Rin Kurohana

Published by Sunny Cabana Publishing, L.L.C.

Printed in the United States of America

Author: Kathy Tennefoss

13-digit ISBN: 978-1-936874-30-9

10-digit ISBN: 193687430X

First Printing

Dedicated to all dreamers out there!

CONTENTS

Meeting Jack

I woke up really early this one particular morning. I think there was too much noise from the wind howling and leafs falling on the roof and then **I** noticed an older man standing at the doorway. He looked familiar but I didn't know his name. This man kept knocking on the door so I thought that he must need help. My parents and sister were sleeping soundly so I decided that I would open the door to see what I could help him with. I was only an eight year old boy but I thought maybe there was something that I could do. I opened the door ever so slightly so that I could peak around the corner. I looked up at this man who was staring down at me. He had a long black trench coat and wore a tan checkered hat with a strange little feather on the side. His eyes were a deep dark brown and he had what seemed like fuzzy caterpillars above his eyes but I really knew they were his eyebrows. Then he smiled from ear to ear. His teeth were perfectly straight and as white as snow.

"Hi," I said. "Is your car broken?"

The strange old man laughed and said, "Hi my name is Jack, No my car isn't broken. I'm your neighbor. I needed someone to help me with some yard work and help me pick some apples in my orchard. Is this something that your parents would let you do sometime?"

"Hi, my name is Addison. I don't know but I think it would be o.k. When did you need help?"

"How about tomorrow morning about 8:30 since its Sunday?"

I was trying not to look too excited when I answered Mr. Jack, "Alright. I will ask my parents."

"Great, I hope to see you tomorrow Addison." "My house is the dark blue one."

I couldn't wait until my parents woke up so that I could tell them about our neighbor Mr. Jack. I love apples! I wonder will he pay me in apples or money. I hope it's both. I started to hear my parents get up. I ran as fast as I could up the stairs and busted into their room.

"Mom, Dad, can I work for the neighbor? Please, can I Please?"

My mom and dad both said, "Calm down let us wake up." We don't even know the neighbor."

"He's really nice. I met him. His name is Mr. Jack."

My mother skeptically said, "What does he want you to do?"

"He wanted help with his apple orchard."

"Please Mom and Dad. I would start tomorrow morning"

"Alright. Alright."

I jumped up and down and said, "Thanks!"

We lived in a small rural town in Ohio in a large two story white farmhouse. We had lots of large oak trees with huge limbs that I would climb on every day. We had all kinds of animals. Two dogs, three cats, some chickens and roosters, and even a few cows. I loved being outside with the animals. I would run and hike all day with my two dogs, Bootsie & Brandi. Bootsie was a black Lab and Brandi was a red Irish Setter with long ears. Bootsie and Brandi protected me from everything. They are the best dogs that anyone could ever have.

We had lots of land or what seemed like lots of land. I even made a tree fort that I could hang out in. It was made of old lumber and a couple of old windows my dad was going to throw away. I would stay out there for hours and hours reading comic books and planning my next adventure. I had my fort fully stocked with ropes, camping lights, carabineers, sleeping bags, and even a Swiss army knife. My dad gave me my first knife on my eighth birthday. I was so excited to finally have my own. It had everything on it! A knife, fork, spoon, magnifying glass, everything to survive!

I kept everything in a backpack all ready to go at a moment's notice. You never know when you will have to escape and it's much better to be prepared.

I almost couldn't wait till morning so that I could go help Mr. Jack. Soon enough it was morning and I was up quick. I ate a huge bowl of cereal and off I was to Mr. Jacks. What would he have me do? Would I get to use a ladder? I hope so. I walked down the hill to Mr. Jacks and knocked on his door. Mr. Jack's house was dark blue with bright white trim with a large front porch with a white porch swing. I grabbed a seat until Mr. Jack came to the door.

> Jack opened the door in a hurry and said, "Come on in Addison."

I was a little scared at first but I didn't want Mr. Jack to see that I was scared at all so I stood up straight and walked right in to his front room. It smelled like fresh cooked bacon, which is one of my favorites so how bad could he be. I walked slowly into the front room and took a seat on the couch. The first thing I noticed is that there was no TV. But there was a huge record player and tons of records lined up on a shelf. His house seemed a bit dusty and old but the record player was really cool. It was larger than our TV. I hope that he shows me how to use it.

I said, "Where is your wife?"

Jack looked up a little sad and said, "She's not with us anymore."

I looked away and said, "Oh." I didn't know what to say after that.

Mr. Jack seemed a bit sad but hustled off to get his coat and ball cap so that he could show me what my chores would be. Mr. Jack was wearing baggy overalls that had white and blue stripes on them. I thought that I needed to get some of those in order to be a professional apple picker.

Mr. Jack headed outside and said, "Come on let me get you some gloves and show you what we are going to do today."

"Alright," I said.

We walked to the back yard and into a very large red barn with lots of horses and a couple of cows. There was hay laying everywhere and all kinds of old tools, saddles, and leather things hanging all over on the walls. It was so big in there. What would I do with all of these tools? I had no idea how to even use the tools. Mr. Jack threw me some gloves and said grab a basket for the apples. I moved quickly to get a basket. I tried to put the gloves on but they were so big that they kept falling off. I wasn't even sure if they were on the right hands but I put them on anyway and out the barn I went.

Mr. Jack went outside ahead of me and jumped on a large red tractor and started it up. It was so loud at first. It sounded like it wasn't running right but he yelled over, "C'mon jump up here Addison." I went climbing up the large wheels and sat down beside Mr. Jack.

"Are you going to show me how to drive this machine?"

"Not yet Addison. Maybe later.
This here machine is one of the
finest pieces of equipment I own.
I can't do anything without this!"

"Ah," I said.

We rode down the hill to where all of
the apple trees were and I hopped down
from the tractor. Mr. Jack turned the
tractor off and followed me to the apple
trees. Mr. Jack was very particular about
how to pick an apple. He wanted to
make sure I was doing it correctly. First
Mr. Jack showed me how to properly
pick an apple. I didn't really know that
there was a proper way to pick an apple.
The apples that are on the outside edges
of the tree are usually riper than the
apples that are in the middle of the
trees. Also it is best to twist the apple so
that it keeps that stem still on the apple.

Mr. Jack said that the apple will last longer and stay fresher longer with the stem still on it. Mr. Jack also wants us to pick through the apples that are on the ground and to make sure there are no insects on them. It is so exciting learning something new. Maybe I will be a farmer one day and have my own garden or my own orchard or better yet my own tractor.

I kept loading up baskets full of apples for a couple of hours now and I have to say I was getting a little tired. Mr. Jack asked if I was hungry and I jumped at a chance to eat lunch. I hopped up on the tractor and we headed back to his house for some lunch. Mr. Jack made peanut butter and banana sandwiches for us. I couldn't believe that he liked my favorite sandwiches. That's so cool! We finished our lunch and headed back out to finish picking for the day.

Now we had to take all of the baskets of apples and store some of them in the cellar beneath Mr. Jack's house. We loaded all of the baskets onto a trailer and hitched the trailer to the tractor and away we went. I hated going into the cellar. It was scary, dark, and cold. Mr. Jack stood at the top of the cellar door and would hand me the baskets so that I could walk down into the cellar. The first time I went down there I was terrified. I ran as fast as I could into the dark cold cellar. It seemed like so many trips but I was really fast. I didn't want to run into any rodents or any other small four legged creatures.

When we were done we sat on the front porch and Mr. Jack made us some lemonade and we sat there and talked about apples and space aliens. Yes space aliens. Mr. Jack kept asking me if I believed that there were space aliens and I didn't want to make him feel bad so I said sure, you know how old people get. It's not like I had ever seen one before.

Mr. Jack paused for a moment and said, "I saw an alien a few times."

I was really excited and said, "Really, where?"

Mr. Jack pointed and said, "Right out there in the apple trees."

"Oh. What did they look like? Where they in a spaceship? What did the spaceship look like? How many were there?"

"Wait, wait, I can't tell you all my secrets."

"Please," I said.

"Maybe tomorrow after school I will tell you more. We have a lot more apples to pick."

"Ah, alright."

Now I was curious. I knew I had to do some research on my own. I needed to know what type of equipment I needed in order to catch an alien or at least battle with one. I had better make a sword or some kind of bow and arrow. I will have to try to sneak one of my dad's flashlights and extra batteries and make sure I keep some beef jerky and dried fruit in my backpack at all times so in case I am out hunting for a long time I will be prepared.

When I got home I immediately went out to my fort and started sketching a design of a bow and arrow in order to fight off the aliens. I needed some really thin wire or small rope and some branches that were flexible and some arrows. I went out to the woods and started to gather the materials that I would need in order to make my bow and arrow. I sat and worked with the material for a while until I came up with a viable working bow. It looked awesome. I used my Swiss army knife to carve the words ***ADDISONS ALIEN FIGHTER***.

Now I had to work on making some arrows. What should I use? I went into my dad's garage and found some pretty sharp stones that I tried to sharpen by rubbing them together to try to form them into an arrow shape. They looked pretty good. Now I needed to find some straight sticks and some wire to attach the sharp stones to the sticks. I cut the sticks into two feet lengths and then started to attach the stones with wire and glue and then I cut the other end so that it would sit just right on the bow wire. It seemed to fit nicely. Now I needed to find some cool feathers. I started looking around the yard and in the trees for any type of feathers to decorate the arrows. I looked and looked until I came upon this bright blue and purple feather laying on one of the oak tree limbs. It was so beautiful and bright. I knew that this was the right feather for the job. It almost looked magical. There were several of them so I could use them on all of my arrows. When I would spin the feathers in the light they would shimmer with gold and silver flakes and they looked different every time, it was as if they were speaking to me saying, "I will save you from the aliens Addison."

I grabbed the feathers and headed down the tree and back to my fort to attach the magic feathers to the arrows. I knew that these feathers would protect me. I attached the feathers very carefully with some very thin leather strips that I found in my dad's garage so that I would not harm the feathers. This was the final touch on my alien fighting machine. I couldn't wait to test it out.

I decided I had better test it out in our back yard first. I don't want to run into an alien and find out it doesn't even work. I went outside and started looking for specimens. I found a squirrel that was lurking about and I thought that's as good as any to practice on. I hid so that the squirrel would not see me creep up on him. I was as still as a mouse and I pulled back the bow and loaded it with my magic arrow and boom it went flying off into bushes. I missed but my arrow flew so perfectly. I think that it was because of that magic feather.

Now I would be ready for anything alien or otherwise. I thought that I had better get some type of protective glasses to wear when I use the bow and arrow. I looked all over my dad's garage and I came across these really cool old fighter pilot goggles that had green lenses. They looked awesome! I also had better make some type of case to carry my arrows in. I looked all over and finally found this really cool old leather bag that would fit my whole alien fighting machine in just perfectly. I also found some silver paint in a old glass jar so I took it out to my fort and started making designs on the outside of the bag. I also painted *ADDISONS ALIEN FIGHTER* on the outside with an outline of my magic feather. I felt like I was ready now. Nothing could stop me now!

I couldn't wait to go explore at Mr. Jacks house but I had better learn more about the aliens from Mr. Jack first. I knew that I had to work with Mr. Jack after school the next day and then I would start asking questions and find out where they exactly were living.

> "Addison, Its dinner time." My mom yelled.

> "I will be right there mom."

We sat and ate dinner and my dad and mom asked me how it went working for Mr. Jack today.

> "It was great. I picked apples all day and Mr. Jack made me lunch. It was fun"

> My mom and dad said, "Great. Are you going to work for him after school?"

"Yeah, until all of the apples are picked."

My mom and dad seemed excited that I had a new job. I was excited that I had a new job. I was more excited that there were aliens involved though. I wouldn't dare tell my parents about the aliens. They would never let me go to Mr. Jack's house if they knew there were aliens there. Plus I don't really think that my parents would believe me if I did tell them.

Meeting the Aliens

Today I was really excited to start the day. I got ready for school and went outside to wait for the bus. I couldn't wait to tell my friend Jaden. We rode the same bus to school. The bus stopped and I jumped on the bus and took my seat. I started to look for Jaden so that I could tell him about the aliens. I saw him sitting in the way back so I waited until the bus stopped at the next stop and then I headed back to where Jaden was sitting and plopped into the seat.

"Hey Jaden I have some really cool news."

"What?"

"Well our neighbor Mr. Jack asked me to work on his orchard this weekend and he wants me to work until all of the apples are picked."

"That sounds cool but you know that Mr. Jacks property is haunted, right."

"What? It's not haunted. It just has aliens."

"Oh that's much better."

"I guess that doesn't sound much better does it?"

"Well I have to work over there today and I will let you know what I find over there."

"You had better be careful because I don't know if it is safe over there."

"Alright,"

Now I didn't know what to think. What if it wasn't aliens but ghosts? I don't have anything to fight off ghosts, just aliens. I hope it's just aliens that I have to worry about.

It seemed like it took forever for school to get done with today. I was waiting in anticipation to start work at Mr. Jacks after school and to have him tell me more about the aliens. The final bell rang and we were off like a bunch of horses running a race. Everyone ran to their busses and hopped on to go home. I could see my stop in the distance and I waited patiently to arrive home. As soon as the bus stopped I jumped up and ran to my house as fast as I could. I threw open the front door and ran up to my room to change into work clothes. I also grabbed my bow and arrow to show Mr. Jack what I had made.

I grabbed a snack and headed down to Mr. Jacks house. I got to his house and looked around to see if anything was lurking about or staring at me before I knocked on the door.

Knock, Knock. "Hi Addison, are you ready for work today?"

I answered anxiously, "Yeah and I even brought my alien fighting machine just in case the aliens come after us."

With his eyes wide opened Jack said, "Wow, let me take a look at that thing. That's really magnificent! That should do the trick if aliens start to bother us."

"Thanks, my friend Jaden said that your orchard was haunted. Is that true?"

"No, I just have aliens."

"Oh, that's what I told Jaden."

"Enough chit chat let's get to work Addison. Here are your gloves. I have the apple baskets already down by the trees."

"Great."

Mr. Jack walked over to the tractor and tried to start it up but it wasn't working. He tried and tried and tinkered with it and I handed him tools and parts but still it wouldn't start. I had noticed that on the outside of the battery that there was this dark purple gook pouring down the side of it.

Quizzically I said, "Look Jack there is purple gook on the battery."

With amazement Jack said, "What purple gook? Oh no. The aliens must be mad because I was talking to you about them."

"Oh no! What should we do?"

"Well we have to be quite. Maybe they saw your alien fighting machine or maybe they heard that you were making one and then they decided to break my tractor."

"I did find some magic feathers in my yard maybe that's what they saw. I'm sorry Mr. Jack. I thought that I could help you with the aliens. I didn't want you to have to fight them by yourself."

I felt awful about making my alien fighting machine. I didn't want them to hurt or sabotage Mr. Jack's equipment. I had better figure out a way to fix this. I decided that I would go and look for the aliens. I started down each aisle of trees searching for anything that looked like an alien. Maybe they would have one eye or skinny legs or big feet. I had no idea. I didn't see anything that would resemble an alien. I even climbed up into the top of some of the trees so that I would be able to see farther and no aliens. I ran back and told Mr. Jack that I didn't see any aliens out there.

"You can't always see them Addison."

Addison was all animated and said, "Oh I thought that they were green with big bulging eyes or maybe even just one eye and large arms and short legs."

"They aren't always green Addison. Sometimes they are purple or blue. They are hard to see because they try to blend into the scenery. I have only really seen them a couple of times and as soon as they saw me looking at them they took off. I think that they live in the ground somewhere."

Addison grabbed a shovel and said, "Well let's start digging then. They have to be around here somewhere. We need to have a talk with them."

"Shhh, you have to be really quite to catch an alien."

I couldn't stand waiting anymore. I had to go investigate some more. I tip toed around every tree until I noticed a purple slime trail on the ground. I followed it until I got to a huge pile of it under a large apple tree. "Wow I found them!" I walked over to the purple slime and kneeled down to take a closer look when the purple slime slid into the ground further. I tried to catch it but it was way too fast. I didn't think about the aliens being slimy so my bow and arrow was almost useless now. I looked at the ground where the purple slime went and I noticed what appeared to be a really tiny door handle. Could that be? A door handle in the ground? I looked around to make sure it wasn't a trap. I grabbed the metal door handle and tried to lift what appeared to be the grass right up. I tried and tried and then finally the ground lifted up just a tad so that I could see into the earth. I kept looking and looking and all that I could see were all of these glowing eyes looking at me. They looked like fire flies on a summers night all moving around and blinking on and off. I wondered if they could see, hear, or smell me. I tried to be super quite but so did they. Then one of the pair of eyes came towards the crack in the open door and said hi to me. How do they know our language or maybe they are English speaking aliens? Are there such things?

In a shaky voice I said, "Hi, I'm Addison. What is your name?"

The purple alien said, "I'm Paris."

I shook my head and said, "Paris, what kind of name is that?

"It's what my parents call me."

"Oh that's cool. What do you look like? Can you come out from the ground? Why do your people keep breaking Mr. Jack's things?

Paris said, "I have to finish my homework and eat dinner first and then maybe I can play."

I had a hard time believing that this alien had parents and homework. It all seemed a bit strange to me. I have never heard of aliens having homework. But I have heard of aliens eating your homework before. My teacher never believed me but now maybe she will.

I was a bit sad because Paris couldn't come out and play but I said, "Alright I can come back later or maybe tomorrow but can you guys fix Mr. Jacks tractor tonight?"

> "I will ask if my parents will fix it but you have to promise not to hurt us. That's why we sabotaged the tractor because we saw you making your alien weapon."

> "Alright .I won't bring my bow and arrow to Mr. Jack's house"

I ran back up to Mr. Jack's house and told him that I had met the aliens and that they would fix his tractor tonight. Mr. Jack didn't believe me. I thought he said he had seen them before. Was he

just kidding around when he was telling
me those stories?

> "Mr. Jack, wait until tomorrow
> and you will see that they are
> real. You will see that your
> tractor will be up and running."

> "Alright, but I think it is really
> broke and I will have to buy a
> new one now."

> "I guess you can go home for
> today and come back tomorrow
> to see if the tractor is working
> and to start picking apples
> again."

> I paused and asked, "Mr. Jack,
> will you tell me more about when
> you saw the aliens?"

> "Sure. It was late one night and I
> was sitting on the porch and

watching what I thought were fire flies flying around. I kept watching and watching but it seemed like there were so many that I couldn't keep track of how many there were. I then noticed in the distance a purple silhouette of a person or what I thought was a person. I kept rubbing my eyes thinking that I was imagining this. This happened almost every night for a week before I got the nerve up to walk towards the apple trees. I got my flashlight and a bat just in case and I headed for the trees and as soon as I would take a step the silhouette would get further away so I just sat there by the tree and watched the silhouette and then more silhouettes joined them and then they started dancing and playing around. It looked like so much fun. They made strange noises and I thought I could only hear them. The sounds were a very high pitch sound, like a song. I didn't know if this is how they talked to each other or what but it sounded so beautiful that I would go out every evening and listen and watch them. It was so comforting listening to them. I guess that is why everyone thought that it was a haunted place because of the sounds that they would make every evening and the little lights. I never did talk to them like you did but I watched every single summer night. It was one of my favorite things to do. I felt safe when they were here dancing and singing in my orchard."

"That sounds so nice. I bet since its fall they are living and dancing in the ground because it is warmer down there."

"Yeah I bet that's it. I always waited till summer to see them and now you have found them in the ground and I can watch them in the winter. That's great!"

I was so excited to share this great news with Mr. Jack and to have friends that were aliens. No one will believe me that I have aliens as friends so I will have to make sure only Jack and I talk about this together. We don't want people to start talking bad about us.

I told Mr. Jack that I had never seen an alien before. I didn't even know they were purple. I can't wait to hear what they have to say. I have so many questions to ask them, like what kind of spaceship do they have? Where do they go to school? Is it an alien school or do they transform their bodies into human figures? What kind of food do they eat?

Mr. Jack seemed really relieved that we had experienced the aliens together. I think he thought he was losing his mind a bit. Mr. Jack never told anyone about the aliens for fear that they would lock him up. Now there were two believers! Maybe the aliens will take me and Mr. Jack on a ride in their space ship. That would be awesome! I will have to ask them tomorrow.

> Mr. Jack said, "Well I guess you had better get home for tonight and I will see you tomorrow and hopefully the aliens will fix my

tractor so that I can get all of
these apples picked.

"They will Mr. Jack, They will."

So off to my house I went. I was a little
mad that I didn't get to meet the aliens
but maybe tomorrow. They seemed so
interesting. I got home and decided that
maybe I should rethink another weapon
just in case they were not friendly aliens.
Now I know that they are slimy and a
bow and arrow won't work but maybe
something else would. I went out to my
fort and started thinking of what to
make and then I went into my dad's
garage to see if there was anything that I
could use to make another alien fighting
machine. So what kills slime? Maybe a
special light ray would work. I gathered
all of the flashlights that I could find
and some duct tape and found an old
broken broom handle. I took each

flashlight and made sure it would turn on and off correctly and the ones that didn't work I found more batteries for them. I then took the flashlights and started to duct tape them all together so I would have one huge flashlight. I had to think of a way to turn all of these flashlights on at once so I tried to wire them all together into one. It seemed to work pretty good. I then found this one flashlight that would flash on and off red lights so I took that one and put it on top so that it would give some extra color to my alien light machine. I duct taped everything together and then I took the broken broom handle and attached it with more duct tape and some old rope my dad had and boom it was done. Nothing would sneak up on me now. I had my alien fighting machine and now my alien light machine. The alien light machine was a bit heavy so I made a large leather strap and tied it to the sides of the broom handle so that I could wear the alien light machine around my shoulders. Now I was set. I hope that the aliens didn't see me make this because then they may not fix Mr. Jacks tractor. I bet they didn't. I was really quite and really careful about making any noise.

It was time for me to come into the house and eat dinner and get ready for school so I had to hide my alien weapons so that my parents couldn't find them. They would ask way too many questions if they saw what I was making. I didn't need that. So I hid my weapons in my fort under a bunch of sleeping bags and locked the door.

Meeting Paris

I t was finally the next day and I couldn't wait to get to Mr. Jacks house. After school I ran put my work clothes on and then went out to my fort and grabbed my alien fighting machine and my new alien light machine, just in case. I hid it once I got to Mr. Jacks so I wouldn't scare him.

> Knock, Knock. Mr. Jack opened the door and said, "Come on in Addison."

> So I walked in and asked, "Did you try out your tractor yet?"

> "No. I was waiting for you."

> "Great."

> Mr. Jack grabbed his coat and gloves and said, "C'mon lets go see if that thing will start today."

> "Alright," I said.

So we headed out the door and walked over to the tractor. Mr. Jack jumped up and put the key in the ignition and nothing.

"Shucks." Mr. Jack said as he kept trying the key over and over again.

Oh no, I bet they saw my alien light machine and that's why it's not starting.

Mr. Jack said, "See Addison the tractor won't start. It's totally broken."

I didn't know what to say at this point. I felt bad because I had made this extra alien fighting machine and the aliens probably saw me make it so they didn't want to fix the tractor. I had to fess up to Mr. Jack and tell him that I made another weapon. I was scared that he would be mad but I had no choice.

"Mr. Jack, I hate to tell you this but last night I made another weapon. It's an alien light machine. I did it just in case. I knew that they were slimy and my bow and arrow wouldn't work so I had to make something else to protect us so I made a really bright alien light machine thinking that it would melt them as soon as I would turn it on."

"Addison I don't think that is why they didn't fix the tractor. The tractor is old and just doesn't work anymore."

Boy was I glad he wasn't mad at me for making another alien weapon. I still did feel a little bad. Mr. Jack worked on the tractor for many hours until it was almost dark out. I decided I would head down to the orchard when Mr. Jack wasn't looking. I snuck into the orchard and got my alien light machine and my alien fighting machine. I knew that I would be alone and I didn't want to take any chances. I searched and searched around all of the trees and bushes. I climbed a couple of trees and just sat there quiet so that the aliens couldn't hear or see me. Then I saw what was a flash or a bright light or something moving really fast. It was amazing. I sat quietly there and waited for it to happen again. I decided set up my alien light machine so that I could flash it on if I needed to. Boom, Flash, Lightning Bolt! What in the world is that? It has to be the aliens! They are so quick! How am I going to catch them? I sat there for a bit longer until the whole sky was dancing around with all of these lights and booms and bolts of lightning. It was amazing. I wonder if Mr. Jack can see this amazing light show. There was so much going on I had forgotten that I had left Mr. Jack by the tractor. I still wanted to see if I could try to talk to the aliens a bit to see why they didn't fix the tractor. Then in the next second I saw a purple blob right under where I was sitting in the tree. I looked down at it and it looked up at me. We both stared at each other for what seemed like hours but I know it was only a couple of seconds.

I finally said "Hi."

Then the purple blob said, "Hi this is Paris."

"Oh, glad to see you. I was checking to see why you guys didn't fix Mr. Jacks tractor."

"Well I asked my parents but they said that they thought that you were making more weapons and so they wanted to wait to see what the weapons were first."

"Well I wanted to make sure that you guys were going to do what you said you were going to do. Mr. Jack has to get his apples picked before it gets too cold outside and he needs his tractor. I only made a light weapon. I really didn't think it would hurt you guys but I had to look intimidating just in case."

"Well light does destroy us. That's why we wait until the evening to come out to play."

"Oh, I'm sorry. I will leave it at home next time. Do you think that you could look at Mr. Jack's tractor now?"

"Well sure."

So I hopped down out of the tree and we both walked to where Mr. Jack was.

Well Paris slithered because he was a blob. We were silent the whole way up to Mr. Jack's house. I wasn't sure what to say to Paris. I mean what do you say to an alien? He didn't ask me any questions either. We finally made it to Mr. Jack's tractor and we stopped in front of Mr. Jack and he looked up at both of us and he said, "What is this?"

"This is Paris."

"Oh, Howdy Paris, what brings you to earth?"

I had to laugh because it was such a funny question and I'm sure Paris didn't know what to say.

Paris responded by saying, "Well you will have to ask my parents. They never tell me anything."

"Sounds fair enough. Do you know anything about how to fix this tractor?"

"Yeah I think I could fix it."

Paris pulled out a huge toolbox from his stomach and started tinkering with the tractor. He was all over the tractor. I couldn't even see where it was anymore. There were tools flying around and all kinds of noises going on and then finally Paris slid off the tractor and said. "Start it up."

"Alright" Mr. Jack said.

He jumped up on the tractor and put the key in the ignition and cranked it a couple of times before it started to sputter and spit and finally it was running perfectly.

"Wow thanks. I'm so glad you were able to fix the old tractor. I really need it to finish picking the apple crop."

Paris said, "No problem. I am glad to help."

Well I was pretty happy that I had first of all met and talked to an alien and that he was able to fix Mr. Jacks tractor. I knew that I couldn't help pick apples if we didn't have the tractor fixed. I think Mr. Jack was amazed that I was talking to the aliens. I think he seemed happier that he had some friends though. Mr. Jack seemed lonely and it was nice to see him smile about the aliens.

I walked Paris back to his doorway in the ground and asked him if maybe we could play after I was done helping Mr. Jack pick more apples.

Paris said, "That would be fun. Then I can tell you about how I got here and what we are really doing here."

"Great."

I waited in the apple orchard for Mr. Jack to drive down to meet me by the apple trees. I could see him driving with the apple baskets in the trailer. I was glad to start work because I knew how important it was to Mr. Jack and I needed some new parts for my bike so I wanted to earn some money to repair it. As soon as the tractor shut off I grabbed a few baskets and started picking as many apples as I could and carried them back to the trailer. We worked for a couple of hours but it was starting to get too dark so we knew that we had to stop until tomorrow. I jumped up on the tractor and we headed up to the cellar to unload the apples. I told Mr. Jack that I wanted to go down and see Paris for a little while. Mr. Jack said that was fine and I headed back down to the door in the ground to see Paris. I wasn't sure if I was supposed to knock or pull the door open at this point. It's not like there was a door bell. So I tried to knock on the ground but I thought if someone saw me they would think that I had lost my mind. Who knocks on the ground? As soon as I knocked Paris opened the door and slithered out to meet me.

> "Hi, Paris. I'm glad you can come outside. I have so many questions to ask you. Where are you from? What do you eat? Why are you here?"

> "Well Addison we are from the planet that earthlings call Neptune. We call it Sera. It's

really cold there, too cold for humans to live there and the wind is fierce. You have to have a special body to live in those types of conditions. That's why we look the way we do. We have special pods that we live in so that we don't freeze or get blown away by the super fast wind. It is a very large planet compared to Earth. There are billions and billions of us there. We are made of a certain material that can't be detected from any machines that Earth has. No one knows we are here on Earth but you and Mr. Jack. Our family was going on vacation when our spaceship broke down and now we are stuck here on Earth until we can find the right materials that are necessary to make the ship fly again."

"Wow, I wonder if I could help you with your spaceship. I can try to help you find the materials you need in order to get back to your home Sera. Where is your spaceship?"

"It's invisible to humans. That would be really great if you could help us. We are not really sure what your planet has that will be similar to the parts we need. We may have to build them from scratch. If you can get some copper and bring it back to us that would be really helpful."

"No problem. I will do what I can. I had better go for now because I think it is about dinner time and I don't want my mom to start looking for me. I haven't told her that I met a new friend, an alien. I don't think that would go over well with her."

"Alright. I will see you tomorrow then."

I waved and said, "Bye."

I started walking up to Mr. Jack's house. I couldn't believe that I was friends with an alien. This just didn't seem right and he wants me to help him with his spaceship. I don't think I could tell anyone about this.

As soon as I got to the front porch Mr. Jack was sitting on the swing and said, "So what's up with your alien friend?"

"Well he needs as much copper as you can get. We need to help him repair his spaceship. Do you have any that we can have?"

"Well I can look around the barn and see what I can come up with."

"Great. I better get going. I will see you tomorrow Mr. Jack." And I waived bye.

I ran home really fast and flew open the front door of the house and ran into the kitchen where my mom and dad were and asked if they had any pennies that they didn't want.

Both my parents looked at me strange and said, "Sure you can have the pennies in the jar in our bedroom. Why do you need them?"

"Oh it's for a science project at school."

"Alright. It's about dinner time get ready and wash your hands."

"Alright," I said.

I ran upstairs and grabbed the penny jar and brought them into my room and added what pennies that I had and then went to ask my older sister if she had any pennies she didn't want. I hated asking my sister for anything but I knew it was for a good cause. I went over to my sister's door and knocked.

"What do you want? I'm doing homework."

"I have this science project and I need as many pennies as I can get for an experiment. Do you have any that you can spare?"

"Sure. I will look around my room to see if I have any."

"Cool. Mom said dinner is ready."

"Good I'm starving."

"Me too."

I headed back into my room to see how many pennies I had and hoped that I would have enough to help rebuild their spaceship. Maybe Mr. Jack has more and we can add them all up together and have what we need. I went to wash my hands and then headed downstairs for dinner. It was a quiet dinner. I didn't want to talk too much because my parents can always tell when something is up. Not that they would know I ran into an alien today and that I was helping him fix his spaceship but they would know something wasn't right as soon as I would talk. It seemed like a long day and I still had to do my homework so I headed up to my room to study and do my math homework. I worked on it for a while until I fell asleep.

Pennies & the Spaceship

I woke up for school today and was excited because I knew that after school I would get to go over to Mr. Jacks and help fix Paris's spaceship. My sister gave me a huge jar of pennies she was saving and I had the ones my mom and dad gave me and I put my whole piggy bank in and I had a huge amount of pennies. I hope that Mr. Jack has some to add to the spaceship.

As soon as school was done I ran home and changed my clothes and gathered all of my pennies. I didn't want my parents to see that I was taking them to Mr. Jacks because then they would ask why I didn't use them on my experiment at school. I found the largest backpack I could find and still they wouldn't all fit so I used two backpacks to take to Mr. Jacks. It was so heavy I decided to take my bike this time to his house. I rode up Mr. Jack's driveway, I wasn't riding fast with all of those pennies but at least I didn't have to walk. I jumped off my bike and ran up and knocked on Mr. Jack's door to see if he was ready to pick some apples and to help fix the aliens spaceship.

Jack seemed anxious to help also. He had several huge canning jars filled to the rim with pennies. I plunked my back packs down onto his living room floor and showed him how many I had. He couldn't believe that we had that many pennies to help the aliens.

> "Well Addison lets go see how many apples we can pick today so that we can also help the aliens with their spaceship."

> "Sounds good Mr. Jack."

We both jumped up on the tractor and headed to the apple orchard. We both seemed to be in great moods today. Maybe it's because we were going to help the aliens. It always feels good to help people or aliens whenever you can. We started to pick as many apples as we could and put the baskets into the trailer behind the tractor. We seemed to be working really fast today, which was good because we lost some hours at the beginning of the week. We had a trailer full before we knew it and then we had to take them back up to Mr. Jack's house to unload them into the cellar. I unloaded them quickly and then we had more daylight so we decided to make another run to the orchard to get more apples. I was excited to get more done for the day.

I decided to ask Mr. Jack what he thought the aliens were going to do with the pennies.

> Mr. Jack just stopped what he was doing and put his hand on his head and then he said, "Well I don't know. I thought about that all night. What do you think?"

"I have no idea. I hope we have enough."

We finished our second load of apples and headed back up to the cellar to unload. It seemed like a good day at work today. When we were done Mr. Jack made us some lemonade and we sat on the porch until we could see the aliens twinkling lights come out. We both seemed like we couldn't wait to see what they were going to do with all of these pennies. We sat on the porch swing and just talked about all kinds of things from cars to candy. Mr. Jack said he loved candy I thought that was so cool. Then before we knew it we started to see the twinkling lights start up. They were appearing everywhere. We finished our lemonade and then went into the house to grab all of our pennies. We started to walk towards the twinkling lights and then in the distance we could see Paris start to walk towards us. We were walking slowly because we had so many pennies to carry but then he saw that we had all of these pennies and he was really excited that we had brought them in order for the aliens to get home. We started piling the pennies outside the door in the ground and Paris said, "You guys can come down here to see what we are doing if you want."

I and Mr. Jack looked at each other for a moment and then both of us said, "Sure."

I think we were both scared but we didn't want the aliens to notice that we were scared and we really did want to see what they were doing with all of these pennies. Paris lifted up the door and there were what looked liked thirty or so stairs with what appeared to be dark black long fur on them.

Paris said, "Could you guys take your shoes off. We don't believe in wearing shoes in our house."

So Mr. Jack and I proceeded to take our shoes off. It seemed so strange to take our shoes off outside. We grabbed the bags and jars of pennies and headed down the fur stairs to the ground floor. It was the most amazing place I had ever seen. The long black fur went all over the floors and there were really small purple and blue lights all over. It looked like the night sky. It was so cozy. There was a strange kitchen with a stove that looked like a huge pizza oven and a large counter made of a large tree trunk. There were little jars of what appeared to dried bugs and spices or maybe they were dried and ground up bugs. They were in the most beautiful jars that you could imagine. They had shells and sparkly things all on the outside of the jars and they had little lights inside of them. They had all kinds of carved pieces of furniture. There was this really cool dining room table that was made of what looked like bright purple wood and shined like a new penny. There were little tiny stools that you could sit on and there was this really cool bench that was green with bright yellow fur that you could sit on. There was no television or any computers or anything like that. I could live here for a long time. It seemed like such a great place. Both Mr. Jack and I were looking around with amazement. Then Paris asked if we wanted some tea. I was a little scared what if it was a magic potion that would make us sleep and then they would take us up to their spaceship and fly to their freezing planet of Sera.

I said, "I didn't think that I would have any."

Mr. Jack said "Sure I would love a cup of tea."

Well Paris wanted us to meet his family. He pointed out to everyone and named them all. For some reason they were all names of countries and famous cities like Brussels, Madrid, Barcelona, Pisa, and all kinds. We couldn't keep up and we didn't seem to remember anyone's name other than Paris's. There were so many of them. They were all different colors and so beautiful to look at. They probably thought we were just staring at them the whole time.

Paris and his parents wanted to see how many pennies we had brought them. I ran over to my backpacks and grabbed what I could and gave them to them.

"Where is your spaceship?"

"It's under the ground with us, but it is invisible to humans."

"Oh. That's right."

"What will you do with all of these pennies?"

"Well we have to melt them all down so that we can build a thin shield all around the spaceship. The copper in the pennies gives the spaceship the power it needs to lift off but we need enough to cover the entire ship."

"Oh. That sounds really cool. Do you think that we have enough?"

"I think that we will have enough but we still need more materials that we hope you can help us with."

"No problem. I would be glad to help."

They had this really large kettle that they dumped all of the pennies into and then heated up until everything was melted. They added a few other things that I had no idea what they were and let it simmer for a while.

I knew that it was getting late and I knew that I had better get home because I knew my mom would be calling me for dinner. Mr. Jack said that he would go to. I grabbed my empty back packs and said good bye to my new alien friends. I did ask what other types of materials that they would need and Paris said that they needed extra power for all of the lights on the spaceship. I asked what I could bring him and he said that maybe we could bring as many glass marbles as we could find. I said I

will look around and see what I can find
and off Mr. Jack and I went.

We walked up the fur stairs and
grabbed our shoes and walked back to
Mr. Jack's house.

> "What did you think of the aliens
> house Addison?"

> "Awesome." It was the best place
> that I had ever seen. What did
> you think?"

> "I thought it was absolutely
> beautiful. They are so nice."

Well we need to get as many marbles as
we can for the aliens. That will be
tomorrow's task. I had better go for now
Mr. Jack and I hoped on my bike and
flew home, ate dinner, and then went
scavenging around the house for
marbles. I had a really nice collection

that I had been collecting for several years and some of the marbles were really rare. I think this is just what the spaceship needs in order for all of the lights to start working right. I hope that Mr. Jack has some marbles. Well I better do my homework and get ready for school tomorrow.

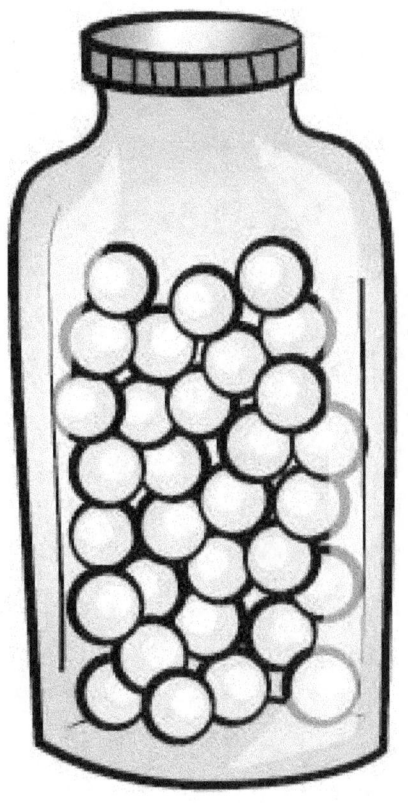

Marbles for the Spaceship

Well today is a new day and I am excited to get to school so that I can ask if any of my friends have any extra marbles. I got ready for school really quickly and ate some cereal and I was off to the bus stop. As soon as the bus stopped I jumped on and ran to the back of the bus where Jaden sits.

"Hi Jaden. How's it going?"

Jaden said, "Good. How's it going working for Mr. Jack?"

I said, "Really good! I love it!" "I wanted to ask you a favor. Do you have any extra marbles that you don't use anymore or that you don't want?"

Jaden looked at me strangely and said, "Why? What are you going to do with them?"

"I am going to make an art project with them."

Jaden said, "Sure you can have my extra ones. I think that I have them in my backpack.

Jaden was digging through his backpack until he came across a small bag of marbles and then handed them to me. I was trying not to look too excited because I didn't want him to start to ask more questions.

Soon we were at school and I had a few minutes before class so I started asking everyone I knew if they had any extra marbles and I was able to come up with a lot more marbles! I was so excited that I hated to be in class today. My backpack was so heavy with all of the marbles that I could hardly lift it but I wasn't complaining because I knew that they were going to be for a good cause.

School seemed to fly by today and I was glad so that I could get home and change into my work clothes and gather all of my marbles. I couldn't help but think what or how the aliens were going to use all of these marbles. Would they melt them like the pennies or would they glue them all over the spaceship? I couldn't wait to see what they were going to do today. I grabbed my heavy backpack and my bike and headed to Mr. Jacks house.

As soon as I got to Mr. Jacks house I ran up to his front door and knocked to see if he was there. I couldn't run to fast with the backpack full of marbles.

> Mr. Jack answered the door and I said really quickly, "Did you find any marbles for our alien friends?"

> "Hi Addison." "I can see that you are really excited to meet and help the aliens today."

> "Yeah." "I gathered a whole backpack full of them."

Mr. Jack tugged at a large bucket that he had on the living room floor.

> Mr. Jack could hardly lift the bucket and said, "I found quite a few marbles myself." I go to a lot of garage sales and I had forgotten that I had picked these up last year." "I am really glad that I can give them a new home."

> I could hardly believe that Mr. Jack had that many marbles. "We will be able to help them out a lot with all of these marbles."

> Mr. Jack grabbed his hat and said, "After we pick apples we can go to the aliens house and give them the marbles."

> "Alright," I said.

I grabbed my gloves and jacket and we jumped up on the tractor and headed for the orchard. We had to use ladders today because the apples we too high for us to grab on the lower braches. It was really fun. We picked for several hours and then loaded up the trailer to take the apples back to the cellar. We were really tired today but we were still excited to talk to the aliens. We sat on the porch to rest for a bit and then Mr. Jack made us some hot apple cider. I had never had that before. It was so delicious! I will have to have my mom make this for me later. I laid on the porch when I was done and kept looking out into the orchard to see if the aliens were starting to twinkle like they do every night but there was nothing yet. I was kind of glad to rest for a bit. We both sat there silent for a good while until we started to see the twinkling lights light up the sky. It was one of the coolest things that I had ever seen and only Mr. Jack and I know about it. It was so awesome that we were the only ones who could experience this. I asked Mr. Jack if he wanted us go and see Paris and he nodded yes. So we headed towards the orchard and Paris's door in the ground with all of our marbles. We were both pretty excited to see our new friends. We knocked on the ground and Paris answered and let us in. We took off our shoes and headed down the fur stairs with all of our marbles.

"Paris it is really good to see you. We were able to gather a bunch of marbles for you. What are you going to do with them?

Paris was really excited and said, "That's so awesome that you were able to gather so many marbles. We are going to take the marbles and place them in the light circuits all over the spaceship so that we will have light and the light shines through the marbles in all kinds of different colors. We don't have any way to get new marbles on our planet. This is going to help us out so much."

I think Mr. Jack and I were grinning from ear to ear the whole time Paris was talking. It was so amazing that we were able to help the aliens out. I never thought that I would be able to do anything like this. I guess it doesn't matter your age or your size you can still make a difference in someone's life.

I asked Paris, "Do you think that we could ever see the spaceship?"

Paris said, "Sure when we get done with fixing it we can take you on a tour of the inside."

"That is so cool. I can't wait to see it!" I asked Paris if he could come outside to play for a little while and he shook his head yes and so we headed up the stairs and outside. We looked around and I asked what he does for fun and he said that he loves to play soccer. I saw a soccer ball in Mr. Jack's barn so I yelled come up here and we can play some soccer. We set up fake goals with sticks and started passing the ball back and forth. Paris was really good at soccer, maybe he can teach me to play better. We played for just a little bit before I realized how late it was and knew that I had to get home for dinner. We walked back to Paris's house and I told Mr. Jack that I had to go home and that I would see him tomorrow. I asked Paris again if there was anything else that he needed for the spaceship and he paused for a long time and then said, "Well we could use as many pens that you have."

I looked at Paris and said,"Pens that you write with?"

"Yeah."

I looked at him funny and asked, "What are you going to use the pens for?"

Paris looked at me and said, "You will see Addison."

"Alright," I said.

So I started to head back to my bike and jumped on and headed home to eat dinner and do my homework.

My parents kept asking me what I did today but I couldn't tell them everything because they wouldn't understand so I just said picked more apples and went to school. I knew we had a large drawer full of extra pens in the kitchen and I asked my mom if I could have all of the extra pens and she said, "What do you need all of those pens for?" I knew that she would start to ask questions. I said that I was working on a project for school in my science class. My mom finally said that I could have them so I grabbed my backpack and scooped all of the pens into it and then ran upstairs to do my homework. I wonder what the aliens are going to use the pens for. It seemed like a strange request but I knew that they had used all of the other items that I brought them so I am sure they will have a good use for all of these pens. I finished my homework and went to bed early because I was really tired tonight.

Pens and the Spaceship

Today I woke up and kept wondering how many more parts the aliens may need for their spaceship. I can't really imagine what the pens would be used for but maybe they don't have pens on the planet of Sera. Either way I found it amusing to see what they were going to use all of these strange parts for.

I got ready for school and caught my bus for school. I sat by Jaden again.

> Jaden asked, "What did you do with all of the marbles?"

> I couldn't tell him about the aliens so I said, "I made an art piece out of it but it didn't really turn out well."

I didn't want him to ask me to look at it because then he would find out that I didn't make an art project.

> Jaden said, "Oh." "When will you be done working for Mr. Jack?"

> I said, "Maybe a week or so more." "I have learned a lot and

plus I am going to save my money for a brand new long board skateboard. I can't wait"

"That's really cool." "Maybe next year Mr. Jack could use both of us."

Jaden said, "Yeah, maybe."

Well soon enough we were at school and I started to scan the floors for extra pens that I could save for the aliens. I found four or five before class started so I thought that was pretty good. I couldn't wait to get to Mr. Jacks today so that I could play soccer and give Paris the pens. It was finally lunch time and I started scouring the floors again for more pens and found several more before lunch was over. Before I knew it school was done for the day and I was off to my house again and to collect all of my pens for the aliens.

I grabbed my bike and backpack full of pens and started heading to Mr. Jacks for an afternoon in the orchard. It was a little cloudy today but at least it wasn't really cold out.

> I ran up to Mr. Jacks door and knocked and Mr. Jack flew open the door and said, "Hi Addison. It's good to see you."
>
> "It's good to see you too!"

I noticed that there was a large gunny sack on the living room floor. I wonder if it was full of pens.

> "What do you have in that gunny sack?"
>
> "Well it's all pens."

"Where did you get all of those pens?"

Mr. Jack was a little sad but answered, "My wife collected them her whole life. She thought that she would use them someday but never used them. So I thought it would be o.k. to use them on this great occasion."

"That's so cool that your wife had saved all of those pens and now she can help with the aliens."

Mr. Jack said, "Yeah it's really good that she saved all of these pens." "Well let's get to picking some apples Addison."

"Alright."

We jumped up on the tractor and headed for the orchard. We didn't talk much when we were picking. We waited until we were done. Mr. Jack wanted to make sure that we got our work done first and then we could have our fun with the aliens. We picked a lot of apples today. They seemed bigger than they were a couple of days ago so they were heavier and harder to hold. I can't wait to take some home to my parents. I love sliced apples and peanut butter sandwiches! We loaded the trailer up and headed up to the cellar to store the apples.

> I asked Mr. Jack, "How many more days until we have picked all of the apples?"

> Mr. Jack said, "Maybe a week. It depends on the weather. I think that if you can work all day on Saturday that will really help a lot. Will you ask your parents if

you can work Saturday and maybe Sunday if you want you can go to the Farmers Market with me and sell the apples?"

"Sure. That sounds really fun. Do you think I could take some apples home this weekend?"

Mr. Jack laughed and said, "Sure."

I couldn't wait to sell apples at the market. We didn't go to the farmers markets too much so I couldn't wait to tell my parents that Mr. Jack wanted me to work at the market. We headed for the porch to rest for a bit until we were going to meet the aliens and give them the pens. Mr. Jack grabbed one of the large apples that we picked and started to slice it up with his pocket knife and gave me some slices. It was the best apple ever! Pretty soon we both saw the twinkling lights start up and what appeared to be music coming from the orchard. I wondered where they were getting the music from or if they were singing. We both got up and headed down to the door in the ground and lugged our pens down the trail. We had a ton of them. I knocked on the door and Paris opened the door.

"Hi Addison and Mr. Jack."

We both said, "Hi."

We took off our shoes and grabbed our bags of pens and headed down the fur stairs. It always looked and smelled amazing in their house. It smelled like mint and was always full of little tiny lights everywhere.

"Wow you guys brought a lot of pens!" Paris said in an excited voice.

"Yeah." "We knew that you needed them so we had a bunch at home and thought that you could use them."

"Boy can we use them."

"What are you going to do with them?"

"Well we have to use them for fuel. We use the ink for fuel. It doesn't take much ink but it's really hard to find on our planet so all of these extra pens will come in handy."

"That's really cool that you use ink for fuel. I can't wait to see the spaceship all done. It will look amazing."

Paris said, "Yeah and maybe you can even take in on a test ride!"

My eyes about popped out of my head and I said, "No way that's awesome!"

I don't think I will sleep all night now. I will be way too excited.

I asked Paris "Do you want to go out and play some soccer?"

"Sure."

So we headed up the stairs and out the door to play some soccer. It was so much fun. We played for a while and then I knew I had better get back home for dinner.

I was curious so I asked Paris, "Hey Paris what do you eat?"

Paris looked at me funny and said, "Well we eat bugs because they are high in protein and we eat grass for our vegetables."

I looked at him and said, "Cool I don't think I would eat either one of those things."

Paris said, "Well back on our planet we eat different things because your planet doesn't have what we normally eat we are adapting to your environment. We normally eat microscopic bugs and organisms that are frozen on our planet."

I said, "Oh I see. It would be scary going to another place and trying to find the same things to eat."

I had to say goodbye now to my new friend and to Mr. Jack because I had to get home for dinner. I had a great time playing soccer and learning about Paris and his customs. I ran back with Paris to his house to say my goodbyes and tell Mr. Jack that I would see him tomorrow. I couldn't wait to get back home to ask my parents if I could work all day Saturday and Sunday. I will definitely have enough money to buy my new skateboard and maybe even some money left to save. I jumped on my bike and rode home and ran into the house.

"Mom, Dad, can I work Saturday and Sunday?"

My mom said, "That's an awful lot of work this week."

"Yeah I know but Mr. Jack has to get the crop in before the weather turns bad and he said he could use some help selling the apples at the farmers market on Sunday. Please mom!"

"Alright"

"Cool."

I ran upstairs to change out of my work clothes and start on my homework. It was nice that the aliens didn't need any more materials today. It sounded like they had everything that they needed for takeoff and Mr. Jack and I get to ride in the spaceship! I can't wait! It will be the coolest thing ever.

I worked the next couple of days after school with Mr. Jack to put away more apples. I didn't play with Paris because he was working on the spaceship with all of the materials that we gave him.

I showed up on Saturday for a full day of work with Mr. Jack. I was pretty excited because I was going to be able to put a full days of work in so that means more money for my skateboard and to fix my bike. We worked all day and Mr. Jack let us take a long lunch with peanut butter and banana sandwiches and lemonade. It was the best! After we were done working for the day I kept a look out for Paris so that I could see if he wanted to play soccer. I saw Paris stick his head out of the door and said that he could play soccer for a while. It was really cool. I had a few extra questions to ask him anyway.

I was kind of sad when I asked, "When are you planning of leaving our planet Paris?"

"I'm not too sure." "I guess in a week because we should be all done putting the spaceship together by then."

"Oh." "That's too bad." "It's been fun hanging out with you and helping with your spaceship."

"I know." I didn't think I would find any earthlings to be my friend." "I have had a lot of fun here and maybe when I get my own spaceship I can come back to visit you."

I was pretty excited and said, "That would be the best thing ever." "You can even teach me how to drive the spaceship."

"Maybe."

"What day can we take the spaceship out with your family?"

"Maybe tomorrow after you come back from the farmers market."

I could hardly contain myself, "That would be so cool." "I can't wait."

It seemed so secretive to sneak around and not tell anyone that I knew these aliens and that I was going to go on a ride in their spaceship. Maybe one day I will tell someone but for now it's best to probably keep it a secret.

I knew that I had to get home for the evening pretty soon so I said good-bye to Paris and Mr. Jack and grabbed by bike ad headed home. I kept day dreaming of what it would be like to fly in a spaceship. Would it be fast or would it be kind of slow and bubbly? I couldn't even really imagine it. Would there will a steering wheel or just buttons that you push? Would there be bedrooms or would it be one open room? I can't wait until tomorrow.

Maiden Voyage

Before I knew it, it was Sunday
and I jumped out of bed quickly
and put on my school clothes
because I would be at the farmers
market and I shouldn't be getting too

dirty today. It will be a great day! I get to go to a really cool farmers market and I get to ride in an awesome spaceship. I bet no one has ever said that sentence before. I ate my cereal and I headed to Mr. Jack's house. When I got there Mr. Jack had most of the apples already loaded up in the truck. Mr. Jack asked if I would go into his house and grab some paper to make some signs for the prices of the apples. So I ran in the house and grabbed some cool pens and some construction paper and went to work designing some signs.

"What price should I use Mr. Jack?"

"They all need to say organic." "These are the different kinds we have: McIntosh, Fuji, Red Delicious, Golden Delicious, and Honey Crisp." "Here are the

prices: McIntosh $1.29 a pound,
Fuji $1.39 a pound, Red Delicious
$1.35 a pound, and Golden
Delicious $1.45 a pound."

Well it looks like my school work is paying off now. I had fun making all of the signs. I had to grab some plastic bags, a couple of fold up tables, chairs, and a scale from the barn and then I think we are ready to go. I saw Mr. Jack go inside the house to grab a small metal box that he was going to use as a cash register. I wonder if he will let me collect the money at the market. I can't wait. I bet I will meet all kinds of people. It looked like Mr. Jack was ready so I jumped into his truck and we headed for the market.

Mr. Jack turned the radio on to some spacey music and he said,

"This is Pink Floyd." "You will like this!"

"It was pretty cool sounding." My dad only listened to country music so it was nice to listen to something different.

Soon enough we pulled up to our little piece of parking lot where we were going to set up. It all looked so amazing. Everyone was running around and grabbing baskets and tables and trying to set up their areas. It was so much fun. I saw a lot of my friends from school and even some of my teachers. I tried to place the correct signs on each of the different baskets of apples and then Mr. Jack said that I could go walk around a bit to see what else was for sale today. I jumped at a chance to see what was out there. I walked around for just a bit. I saw a lady who had lots of cheese. Then there was a couple of people who were selling flowers and then some people who were selling vegetables. The best thing I saw was a booth that was selling hot waffles. The smell was so amazing. I just had to have one. I ran back to Mr. Jack and told him what I found and he said that he would give me an advance in my check and he gave me a couple of bucks to get him and me a hot a gooey waffle. I waited in line and I thought my eyes were going to pop out when it was my turn. There were some with chocolate and some with whip cream and strawberries! Whoa! I ordered chocolate for me and Mr. Jack. I ran back to our booth as fast as I could. This was the best thing ever. I was so excited that I asked Mr. Jack if he could take me to the farmers market every Sunday. We finished our waffles and had to get prepared for the customers. I think we both had chocolate all over our faces but we didn't care. We were joking around and having the time of our lives. We must have seen hundreds of people who wanted Mr. Jack's famous apples. I had no idea he was this famous. I wanted to remember this moment because I think this is what I want to do when I grow up. Maybe Paris will come and live in my orchard when I get older. Mr. Jack said that I would load the apples up into the bags for the customers and he would take their money. It was a great system. We were getting low on almost all of the apples. It was really a lot of fun. It was almost closing time about 1:00 p.m. and Mr. Jack asked me if there was anything from the market that I wanted and I said that I would go look. I saw a really wonderful peach pie that would be really good for dinner so I asked for another advance and Mr. Jack gave me a few bucks to go pick one out. I loved the whole farmers market. It was such a great way to make money and to meet great people.

I started to help Mr. Jack pick up the tables and chairs and what we had left of the apples and then he said that he was going to pay me today for all of my hard work. He added up all of my hours for the last couple of weeks and I had a $154.00. I couldn't believe it. I almost fell over. I had never seen that much money before. I jumped up and down and told Mr. Jack that I can get my new skateboard now. Mr. Jack was pretty excited that I was able to help him and he said that he couldn't wait to see my new skateboard. We headed for his truck and loaded up the rest of the stuff and started to drive back to Mr. Jack's house.

I asked Mr. Jack, "Are you excited to ride in the spaceship today?"

Mr. Jack was trying to pretend that he wasn't excited but he yelled, "Yeah, I can't wait!" "It should be really fun." "I have never ridden in a spaceship before."

"Me either."

"It will be a great adventure," said Mr. Jack.

We pulled into his driveway and unloaded the tables and other various items and then went into the house to get something to drink and cut up an apple to eat while we were waiting for Paris to tell us about our spaceship trip. We sat on the front porch and talked and talked about all kinds of things from tractors to traveling by a sail boat. Mr. Jack said that he had traveled in a sail boat to some islands before. I thought that was really cool. I want to do that some day.

> Before we knew it we spotted Paris walking up to the front porch and he yelled, "C'mon you guys it's time we try out this spaceship."

We both jumped up and ran down the hill to where Paris's front door was. Paris said well we can't show you where it's located so I have to blind fold you both so that you can't come back to look at the spaceship later. We both looked at each other and said sure sounds fun.

Paris carefully blind folded us and then we held on to a rope and he kept saying step by step what to do. Paris would say you are going to be walking up a hill and then down a hill, turn to your right, now turn to your left. We were felling dizzy at this point. We walked for what seemed like a half an hour. Then finally we arrived to this huge open field. Paris said we can take off our blind folds now. So we ripped those things off so fast. We couldn't wait to see what the spaceship looked like.

We both stood there with our mouths wide open and stared at the very large spaceship. We had no idea it would be that large! It had so many lights that were different colors. The spaceship was like a shiny metal round egg with three super long legs that stood on the ground. There were small round windows all in a row around the outside of the spaceship. Both Mr. Jack and I inched up to the spaceship so we could see more of the details. There was a huge hole in the middle of the metal egg that had bright purple lights that were around the opening. We were scared but we both walked slowly under the opening and as soon as we did it opened like a huge eye ball and it said, "Welcome". We must have jumped 200 feet at this point. We both looked up and said, "Hello". We were not sure what to think at this point but we knew that Paris and his family were really nice so they wouldn't take us back to their planet as hostages.

> Paris yelled, "What do you think?"

> We both said, "It looks amazing!" I couldn't wait to take it for a ride.

Paris asked us to stand under the hole where all of the purple lights were so that we could be transported to the inside of the spaceship. So we got lined up and before we knew it we were inside the spaceship. We felt light as a feather inside the spaceship. There were hundreds of lights and gadgets all over the walls. There appeared to be televisions on one wall with pictures of what looked like other planets and of other different aliens. I wondered if this is where we are going to be going today. I hope so! It would be cool to see other aliens and I would love to see different planet.

Paris started to talk in what appeared to be a totally different language to his family and then Paris asked us if we wanted to take a tour of the spaceship. So we jumped at a chance to look all over this spaceship! We walked down these narrow halls that had floors that lit up with bright blue lights. Every time we would step on the ground it would light up right in front of us. There were little tiny doors on the sides of the hallways that were lit up in bright red lights and brightly colored paint. Paris finally stopped at one of the red doors and said lets go in here, he said it was his play room. I couldn't hardly believe what I saw when I walked through the doorway! We walked through this tiny little red stripped door and into the most amazing place that I had ever seen in my entire life. There were huge swing sets, merry go rounds, 200 feet water slides, hot air balloons, small cars, horses, bikes, and monkey bars. The place was all done with tons of different color lights and was one of the most magical places that I have ever set eyes on. Paris said we could play with anything we wanted to. Both Mr. Jack and I ran to see every little thing we

could before the spaceship took off. We
both ran for the purple hot air balloon. It
looked like so much fun. We jumped
into the basket and Paris showed us
how to fly it and we were off. Here we
were flying in a hot air balloon inside a
spaceship! It didn't seem possible! From
the air we could see so much more!
There were all kinds of booths where we
could get fluorescent cotton candy, hot
pretzels, waffles, and bright red candy
apples! We couldn't wait to try them!
We flew around for a bit but we knew
we didn't have much time because we
had to get ready for the journey. We
landed the hot air balloon and ran for
the candy apples and then Paris said we
had to get prepared for flight. I hated to
go because I was having so much fun
but I also wanted to see what was out
there in the universe. Paris said to
follow him to the next room so we could

get dressed into our flight suits. We walked into this room that had all of these strange suits hanging on the walls. They were bright lime green and had silver stripes all over them.

> Paris said, "Grab a suit that fits you and put it on so we can take off soon."

So we did. It was strange putting this tight bright green suit on. I hope that when we go to this other planet they won't think that I am an alien. It was like wearing pajamas with feet in them. Both Mr. Jack and I were cracking up laughing at each other dressed in these strange suits. Then we followed Paris to the front of the spaceship were we first were transported. There were tall black seats all in a circle around all of these strange gadgets and lights. We took a seat and strapped ourselves in really tight. We didn't know how fast this spaceship could go. Paris said that we are just going to take a short trip to the planet Zelco. I was like oh yeah Zelco….. He said it would only take several minutes. I almost couldn't believe it. I closed my eyes and all I could hear were buzzes and high pitch sounds going on and off and before I knew

Paris yelled. "We are here."

"Great!"

I couldn't wait to see where we were. Paris said that if we go outside that we had to keep the suit on so that it would protect us from the elements. We could see on all of the television screens that there were strange beings outside but we still wanted to get out and see what it was like or what the temperature was like. Paris didn't have to wear a suit because he is already an alien and he could protect himself. Paris said that we had to stand near the doorway so that we could be transported to the outside.

Before we knew it we were all outside. There were strange little beings all different colors and only about a foot tall running around all over the place and speaking a really strange language. Their heads were larger than their bodies and they all had long curly blond hair. I think Paris could understand them but he never really said too much to them. There were hardly any trees or grass on this planet. All that it had was huge fluorescent pink lakes and the little beings kept jumping in and out of the lake. Maybe it was the weekend and they were just all hanging out. It looked amazing though. Paris said that we could go for a walk around and explore for a while if we wanted so we started out on our journey. There was a strange smell in the air almost like burnt popcorn or something like that. It made me hungry but we kept walking around the lake and taking it all in. We had never seen a place like this before so it was strange. We thought that Earth was the only place to live and here we were with other beings on another planet. It was amazing and beautiful. As we were walking we ran into this very large purple tree that had these strange little berries on them and the little aliens were eating them. I thought that it would be alright to take a few and eat them along the way but within a few minutes I started to change color.

Mr. Jack looked at me very panicked and said, "What did you do?"

I looked at him and said, "I ate a few of those berries."

Mr. Jack said, "You're turning blue." We had better run back to the spaceship to ask Paris for help."

As soon as we got there Paris started laughing hysterically at me and said, "The blue color will wear off soon, don't worry."

I was really grateful that I wasn't going to stay blue. What would my parents say! We knew that Paris was waiting for us so we said that we could go now. We were transported inside of the spaceship and as soon as we got inside everyone started to laugh at me because I was blue. It was really kind of funny. I had never been blue before but it eventually wore off.

 Paris said that we were going to look at other planets but the other planets were toxic to humans so we could only look on the televisions to see what was out there. We strapped ourselves in the seats and off we were to another planet. The next one was even stranger. It had bright orange trees everywhere and what appeared to be bright red snakes with bulging eyeballs all over the ground. The next planet had nothing but snow and no people or I mean aliens. Then Paris said that we had better get us back to Earth before it gets too late.

It has been such an amazing day. I will never forget the things that I have seen or the aliens that I have met. Before we knew it we were back on Earth. We took our suits back to the suit room and we knew that we had to go but we didn't want to. We wanted to stay and travel and play.

> Before I knew it Mr. Jack had looked at Paris and said, "Do you think that I could fly with you full time?"

> Paris didn't know what to say. "What about your orchard and your life here on Earth?"

> Mr. Jack said, "I am going to give my orchard to Addison to take care of and I will visit him all of the time."

> Paris said, "Well if you really want to fly with us all over the universe I guess that would be fine."

I couldn't believe that Mr. Jack wanted to give up his apple business to me or that he really wanted to fly in a spaceship fulltime. I would take really good care of the orchard for him.

>Mr. Jack looked at me and said, "Are you sure you want to take care of my orchard?"

>I said, "I would love to!"

>Mr. Jack said, "I will be back every few weeks to check on it and you and to see if you have any questions."

What would I tell my parents? I guess I could just tell them that Mr. Jack is traveling to another country and that he is paying me to look after his orchard. That would be a great answer! Plus I could always see the aliens every time Mr. Jack would come back so I could always be friends with Paris and take spaceship rides every time they would come back. That would be perfect! I would do that until I graduated and then I could go on long trips with Paris too!

Jack Leaving

We arrived back on Earth but I was a little sad because it seemed like I was leaving my best friends. I know that I will get to see them sometimes but it wasn't the same as hanging out with them every day.

Mr. Jack had asked if he could stay a few days to prep me for running the orchard and also for time to pack a few of his belongings. Paris said that would be fine but then they had to be on their way to another planet for and exploration trip.

Mr. Jack and I went into the house where he started to write everything down for me on how to grow apples and what time of year I should trim the trees and all sorts of stuff. I knew it would take him a while so I asked if I could go home for the day and then I would be back early in the morning. Mr. Jack said that would be great.

"It sure was a great day and now I will be able to see all kinds of planets every day."

I said, "I know. I can't wait for you to tell me more about what is in the universe!"

I told Mr. Jack good bye for the night and headed home. I was smiling from ear to ear when I opened the front door. I had the most amazing day but I couldn't tell anyone because then they would know I was hanging out with aliens. I ran into the kitchen to tell my parents about how Mr. Jack wants me to take care of his orchard while he is traveling to Europe. They were not too sure about it but I told them that I could use the extra money for college and then they were in! I told them that Mr. Jack was writing up a plan for how to take care of the orchard for me. They seemed like it was a lot for me to do but I told them how much fun I had at the Farmers market and how that I may someday want to be a farmer and this would give me the skills that I would need. They couldn't believe that I wanted to be a farmer but they said that would be fine for now as long as my grades didn't fail. I was so excited that I could hardly contain myself. This has been the best year ever! I have learned how to take care of apples, set up for farmers markets, meet aliens, ride in spaceships, and best of all meet Mr. Jack!

The next morning I was up early and ready to go over to Mr. Jacks so that he could teach me more about the apples. I took my bike over to Mr. Jacks and knocked on his door. Mr. Jack came to the door and he seemed really excited to see me and to show me about the apple trees. He grabbed his list, hat, and coat and we headed out to the orchard. Mr. Jack was talking about everything from what to feed the trees to when to water them. It was fascinating. I learned so much!

Then I asked, "How will I get a hold of you if I need to ask a question?"

Mr. Jack look puzzled and said, "I'm not sure I guess go to the orchard at night and see if you can see the lights from the spaceship. You could also hang a note on one of the trees and I will try to answer your question in case you can't make it over to the orchard."

I said, "That sounds like a great idea."

After Mr. Jack showed me everything that I needed to know Mr. Jack said that he had a secret hiding place inside the barn where he kept extra money just in case I needed it for supplies for the orchard. We walked into the barn and climbed up a ladder unto the top floor of the barn and then I saw this little tiny refrigerator. Mr. Jack opened the refrigerator and took out a large box of what looked like cereal but when he opened the top of the box and showed me what was in it, it was full of 100 dollar bills! There were probably 10 or 12 cereal boxes in the refrigerator. I was trying not to act like it was a big deal but I couldn't imagine that.

> Mr. Jack said, "Now if anything happens to me in the spaceship this refrigerator and this apple orchard is yours!"

I took a step back and said, "Are you sure you know what you are talking about. That's a lot of money and a lot of apples Mr. Jack."

Mr. Jack said, "I trust you will take care of the land if it needs taking care of and I really want you to have it because what am I going to do with the orchard when I'm in space?"

I said, "Well I guess I can take care of it till you get back."

I was floored that Mr. Jack would put me in charge of something as important as growing his apples. Mr. Jack made me promise that I would not tell a single soul about the refrigerator or about him giving me the orchard to take care of. I knew that I would never say a word to anyone because then I would have to say that Mr. Jack was flying around in a spaceship with aliens. That's not really a great way to open a conversation.

Jack and I went back to the house and I then I started to help him pack his bags for the spaceship.

> Mr. Jack said, "Do you think I will need a lot of stuff there. I should have asked Paris what to pack."

> I said, "I don't think you will need much because they have space suits and all the candy apples you can eat on the spaceship!"

> Mr. Jack, "You're right! What was I thinking?"

Soon it came time to meet up with Paris and to say good-bye to my friends. I was a little sad but I knew that they would be back soon and I had a huge task of taking care of the orchard. We waited until it was dusk outside and then we started to see Paris and his family dance around in the lights and that's when we knew it was time to meet. I walked with Mr. Jack and helped him carry his bags to the spaceship. The spaceship was really lit up this particular night. I hugged Mr. Jack good-bye and said my good-byes to Paris and his family and said that I would see them really soon. Mr. Jack stood under the spaceship where he knew he would be transported to the inside of the spaceship.

> Mr. Jack yelled, "Take care of the apples and I will see you really soon."

I yelled back, "I will and make it back safely!" and they were off just like that!

I couldn't help but feeling a bit jealous because I wish I was going with them but I knew I would eventually get to go with them and I needed to finish school and help with the apples so that Mr. Jack could take this fascinating journey to other planets! Mr. Jack deserved to go. He has worked his whole life at the orchard and he wanted to explore new territories! Plus when he gets back he will tell me all of his great adventures!

The End

About the Author

Kathy is the author of the ADDISON ADVENTURE SERIES, MY SUMMER IN A SILVER COCOON, AWESOME RAW FOOD GUIDE, 80 AWESOME RAW FOOD RECIPES YOU CAN'T LIVE WITHOUT, THE VIVACIOUS VEGAN, THE VIVACIOUS VEGAN DESSERTS, THE VIVACIOUS VEGAN TIKI PARTY, and many short books on raw food, but her favorite thing to write is children's fiction adventure books. Kathy was inspired by her nephew and his great love for stories! He just couldn't get enough!

Kathy is considered a traveler, health-nut, and yoga lover at heart!

She was born in Ohio and moved to Oregon where she finished her Physical

Anthropology degree and then to Florida where she finished a Culinary Arts degree and now lives any place where she can write!

SunnyCabanaPublishing, L.L.C.

Email or Fan Email:
SunnyCabanaPublishing@gmail.com

All books are also available on kindle, nook, and I-bookstore!

Addison Adventure Series